Written By
Neil Gaiman &

Illustrated By
Adam Rex

Chu's First Day of School

HARPER
An Imprint of HarperCollinsPublishers

For Ronan.
–N.G.

For Jack.
–A.R.

Chu's First Day of School   Text copyright © 2014 by Neil Gaiman   Illustrations copyright © 2014 by Adam Rex
All rights reserved. Manufactured in China.
No part of this book may be used or reproduced in any manner whatsoever without written permission
except in the case of brief quotations embodied in critical articles and reviews.
For information address HarperCollins Children's Books, a division of HarperCollins Publishers,
10 East 53rd Street, New York, NY 10022. www.harpercollinschildrens.com

Library of Congress Cataloging-in-Publication Data
Gaiman, Neil.
Chu's first day of school / Neil Gaiman; illustrated by Adam Rex. –First edition.
pages cm
Summary: On the first day of school, a young panda learns about the special
things his animal classmates can do.
ISBN 978-0-06-222397-5 (hardcover bdgs) [1. First day of school–Fiction. 2. Ability–Fiction.
3. Pandas–Fiction. 4. Animals–Fiction.] I. Rex, Adam, illustrator. II. Title.
PZ7.G1273Ch 2014
[E]–dc23 2012050676

The artist used oil and mixed media on board to create the illustrations for this book.

Typography by Alison Carmichael 14 15 16 17 18 SCP 10 9 8 7 6 5 4 3 2 1 ❖ First Edition

There was a thing
that Chu could do.

Chu was worried. He had never been to school before.
"What will happen?" Chu asked his father. "Will they be nice?"
"They will be nice."

"Will they like me?" Chu asked his mother.
"Of course they will like you," she told him.

Chu hoped they were right.

After breakfast his parents took him to the school.
There were other boys and girls there.

The teacher
had a
friendly face.

She showed them where the toys were,
and where they would sit.

"Now," she said, "I want each of you to
tell the class your name, and I will write it
down on the blackboard. You must say one
thing that you love to do."

"My name is Jengo.
I like to get things down
from high places.
What do YOU do?"

Chu didn't say anything.

"My name is Pablo. I love to climb up things.
I can climb trees, if they are not too big.
What do YOU do?"

Chu didn't say anything.

"My name is Robin.
I can sing and I can fly.
I love to sing.
What do YOU do?"

Chu didn't say anything.

"My name is Tiny.
I like to go into my room and close the
door and not come out until I want to.
What do YOU do?"

One by one they went around the whole class.
They all had something special that they did.
They loved to dance, or to be funny,
or to run very fast, or to read books,
or to hang upside down.

The teacher wrote each name on the blackboard in chalk.
She needed more space to write.
She rubbed out things that had been on
the blackboard before.

There was a lot of
chalk dust in the air.

Now only one person was left.
"Hello, little panda," said the teacher. "Tell us about you."

"My name is Chu."

AAH-

AAAAH-

AAAAAH-

AAaachoooO

"That's what I do."

"How was school?" asked his father.
"It was pretty good," said Chu.

"Did they like you?" asked his mother.

"They liked me," said Chu.
"They were nice.
I'm not worried anymore."

Goodnight.